WHITNEY CLIMBS THE TOWER OF BABEL

and learns what happens to snobs

THERESE JOHNSON BORCHARD
ILLUSTRATIONS BY WENDY VANNEST

PAULIST PRESS
NEW YORK / MAHWAH, N.J.

Library of Congress Cataloging-in-Publication Data

Borchard, Therese Johnson.
Whitney climbs the Tower of Babel and learns what happens to snobs / by Therese Johnson Borchard ; illustrations by Wendy VanNest.
p. cm.—(Emerald Bible collection)
Summary: Having shown a proud and arrogant attitude about her soccer team's winning streak, Whitney is transported by her emerald Bible back to Biblical times, climbs the Tower of Babel, and discovers what happens to snobs.
ISBN 0-8091-6675-5
1. Babel, Tower of—Juvenile fiction. [1. Babel, Tower of—Fiction. 2. Pride and vanity—Fiction. 3. Soccer—Fiction. 4. Time travel—Fiction.] I. VanNest, Wendy, ill. II. Title. III. Series.
PZ7.B64775 Wc 2000
[Fic]—dc21

00-056496

Published by Paulist Press
997 Macarthur Boulevard
Mahwah, New Jersey 07430

www.paulistpress.com

Printed and bound in the United States of America

The Emerald Bible Collection
is dedicated
to the loving memory of
Whitney Bickham Johnson

Table of Contents

Prologue

Nana's Emerald Bible

It was a warm August morning the day the Bickham family moved from their Michigan home to a residence in a western suburb of Chicago. Mr. Bickham's mother, Nana, who had lived with the family for some time, had passed away in February of that same year. Not long after, Mr. Bickham landed a great new job; however, it meant the whole family would have to leave everything that was familiar to them in Michigan and start again in Chicago.

It was especially hard on Whitney and Howard, the two Bickham children. They had grown accustomed to their school in Michigan and had several friends there. They didn't want to have to start over at a new school. Whitney, especially, was heartbroken about moving away from Michigan, for Nana's death alone had been very difficult on her. For Whitney, the Bickhams' Michigan home was filled with wonderful memories of Nana that she did not want to leave behind.

Nana and Whitney had had a very special friendship. Since Mrs. Bickham worked a day job that kept her very busy, it was Nana that had cared for Whitney from the time she was a baby. Growing up, Whitney spent endless hours with Nana. Her most wonderful memories of Nana centered around those afternoons when the two would go down to the basement and read stories from the Bible. Nana would sit on her favorite chair and read a story to

Whitney that related in some way to a problem Whitney was having. As Whitney sat on her grandma's lap listening to the story, her own situation always became a little clearer.

When Nana became sick and knew she was going to die, she called Whitney into her room and said:

"Dear Whitney, you know how special you are to me. I want you to have something that will always bring you home to me. I have a favorite possession that I'd like to leave with you—my Emerald Bible. Every time you open this special book, you will find yourself in another world—at a place far away from your own, and in a time way before your birth. But I will be right there with you."

Nana was so weak that she could barely go on, but, knowing the importance of her message, she pushed herself to say these last words:

"Whatever you do in the years

ahead, keep this Bible with you, as it will help you with all of life's most difficult lessons. And remember, when you open its pages, I am there with you."

As Nana closed her eyes to enter into an eternal sleep, Whitney spotted the beautiful Emerald Bible that lay at Nana's side. It sparkled like a massive jewel, and on its cover were engraved the words, "Lessons of Life."

And so it began that Whitney would take her Emerald Bible to the basement of the new home and, sitting on Nana's favorite chair, would look up to heaven and ask Nana to help her choose a story to read.

CHAPTER ONE

UNDEFEATED

As Central Middle School's star soccer player, Whitney Bickham had much practicing to do before the national championship, five days away.

Coach Smith had warned the team against becoming overly confident. He sensed the attitude of superiority that was spreading among the players like an epidemic. The more victories the team acquired, the more often he heard the girls say that they were unconquerable, impossible to beat.

This made Coach nervous. He had learned long ago that you can never be too sure of anything, and if you are, it will end in disappointment.

However, the team was having fun with their winning streak. As members of the only undefeated team in their division, all of the girls wearing the green and gold soccer uniform were respected like royalty of the sports community, heroines of the field. It got to their heads, and to some more than others.

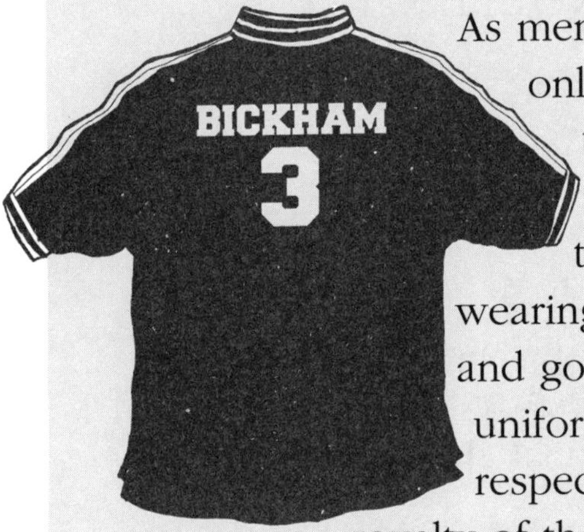

It was Monday before the big game. A half hour after practice was scheduled to begin, half the team was still missing. At forty-five minutes after the hour, Coach Smith paced the field, baffled as to how he was going to bring back the humility and discipline that

had taken the team to success.

Finally Coach heard the voices of several players in the distance. Whitney and a couple of her soccer friends were laughing and giggling as they sluggishly approached the soccer field, oblivious that Coach Smith and the others were waiting for them to begin practice.

"Hey, guys," Whitney yelled out, "do you think if we played this game without our goalie that the Ravens would have a shot at winning?"

The other two girls laughed, contributing their own sarcastic comments.

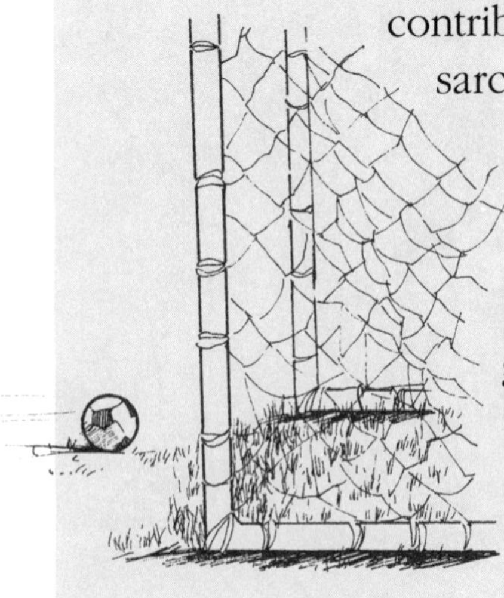

"What if we scored a goal or two for them, just to keep the game going?" Nicki added.

"Maybe we should wait until

the fourth quarter to score any goals, just to psyche them out," Tonya schemed.

"Girls, hurry up!" Coach Smith screamed from the field. He was visibly upset. Whitney, Nicki, and Tonya stopped joking around and ran to the field.

He asked the team to huddle together, and by the tone of his voice, everyone knew that he was really angry.

"I've had enough of your attitude and behavior. Yes, we've had our share of victories, and right now we stand undefeated. But how do you think we got there? By showing up late for practice? By making fun of our competition? By convincing ourselves that we are so good that we don't need to practice?

"Absolutely not, girls. I'm disappointed that you have given up the discipline and hard-working spirit that

this team was made of at the beginning of the season."

There was silence. For the first time in a long while, the team realized that they needed a lot of practice in order to compete well on Saturday. They were embarrassed that they had become so proud and arrogant.

Coach called off practice for the day and asked everyone to go home and think long and hard about what he had said.

"If any of you think you don't need practice, I don't want you on the team. I'd rather have a couple of struggling kids who work hard at this game than some gifted players who think they know everything."

Whitney, Tonya, Nicki, and the other star players sullenly walked away from the field. Without saying a word, each went her separate way.

Usually Whitney left soccer

practice happy and uplifted. Coach always gave her positive feedback and told her how important she was to the team. But this time she was part of the problem. She was sure she had let him down, and she was disappointed in herself.

Mrs. Bickham, who had taken the afternoon off from work, was surprised to see Whitney home so early. Just a half hour earlier, the ten-year-old couldn't wait to run off to soccer practice with her friends. Whitney seemed happier than ever before, or at least the happiest Mrs. Bickham had seen her daughter since the family's move from Michigan.

However, the same carefree girl who impatiently slammed the door behind her on her way to practice less than an hour before tried to sneak quietly inside her home without being noticed.

Had Mrs. Bickham not been in the living room reading, she wouldn't have heard anyone come through the door. But since she was there, she went to the door to greet Whitney.

Tears dribbled down the sides of Whitney's red cheeks. Before Mrs. Bickham could ask what was the matter, Whitney blurted out, "I don't want to talk about it."

There was only one person in the world that Whitney could open up to, and that was her grandmother, Nana. Since Nana's death, Whitney would go down to the basement and sit on her late grandmother's favorite chair and read a story from her most precious treasure . . . her Emerald Bible.

Whitney's pup, Bailey, was already sitting on Nana's favorite chair, waiting for story hour to begin. The golden lab had been through the routine often enough to know what was going to happen. He was excited about his new adventure.

Before Whitney reached for the Bible hidden underneath the chair, she took a deep breath, looked up to heaven, and said, “Nana, read me a story this afternoon. Choose a story of wisdom for me.”

The ten-year-old remembered the words Nana spoke to her just before dying:

"Whatever you do in the years ahead, keep this Bible with you, as it will help you with all of life's most difficult lessons. And remember, when you open its pages, I am there with you."

Rays of light emerged as Whitney gently opened the emerald cover. Its radiant green color shone as brightly as the day Nana gave it to her. She thumbed through its delicate pages until her eyes stopped at a certain paragraph. She began to read aloud . . .

"The descendants of Noah grew in number, but they all spoke the same language. For many years they wandered about in the lands of the east. Eventually they came upon a wide plain in the land of Shinar, where they settled."

CHAPTER TWO

THE TALL TOWER

As soon as Whitney looked up from reading the paragraph, she found herself in a very interesting land. She was not on a ship in the Mediterranean Sea, as she had been in the story of Noah and the whale. No massive boats around, like the one she boarded with Noah's family. And so far she hadn't seen a giant like the one David fought.

The closest thing in comparison that she could think of was Solomon's grand temple. For in front of her this time was a gigantic tower, so tall that it pierced the clouds above it and Whitney could not see where it ended.

"Could it be possible that this tower is higher than the Sear's Tower back in Chicago?" Whitney wondered. If she could see as far as Michigan and Wisconsin at the top of the modern skyscraper, she could only imagine what all she would be able to see at the top of this thing.

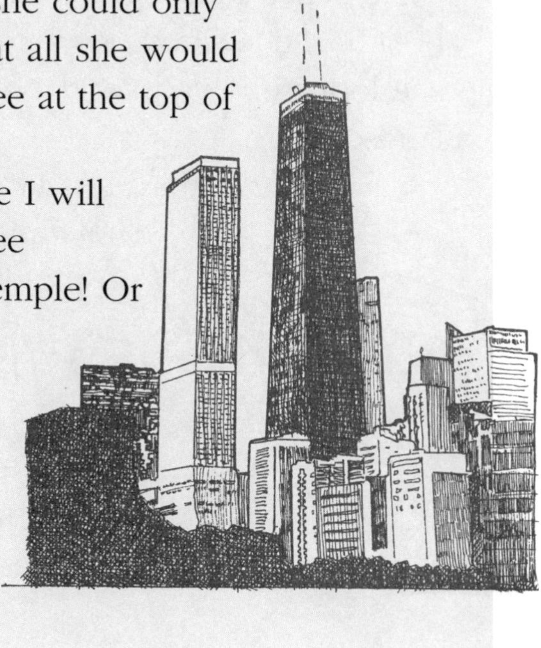

"Maybe I will be able to see Solomon's temple! Or Noah's big boat!" The possibilities for seeing her friends in different biblical lands were endless. But the ten-year-old had her timelines all confused and didn't quite know how the stories fit together.

In her wonderment, Whitney barely noticed Bailey dart off to the tower's first floor of stairs. Without hesitation she ran after him like a cop chasing after a band of robbers. He had made it up three flights of stairs before she reached him. Completely out of breath, she secured her hold on him as she looked down over the arid landscape.

From the third terrace of the tower she could see people in the distance making mud bricks. To her it looked like millions and millions of fudge bars

baking in the sun. The bricks were perfectly molded blocks of mud and straw. And there were fields and fields of them wherever she looked.

Whitney wished they smelled like fudge bars, too. Instead, she was hit by a horrible cementlike smell from the boiling pots of tar, which was used as plaster between the mud bricks.

"These people are really organized!" Whitney thought to herself. She laughed as she compared the efficient process below her to the last-minute shuffle of Noah's family assembling the humongous ark.

Never before had the young girl seen such precision in the construction of a building. The tower resembled the incredible pyramids of Egypt that she saw when she traveled there with Joseph's brothers. The base was wide, the structure narrowing with each terrace.

Little did she know that the workers beside her were Noah's descendants who had devised techniques for brick architecture.

Whitney was determined to find out where she was so that she could look it up on her modern map at home.

She turned to the man beside her who was laying bricks. He was dressed in a simple wrap around his waist. No shoes. Nothing on his chest. Yet he was sweating as though he were dressed in a wool winter coat.

And he appeared to be somewhat annoyed by her interruption.

"I am terribly sorry to bother you, sir," she began. "I was just wondering if you would be so kind as to tell me the name of this tower."

The man looked at her as if she had just asked the world's dumbest question. But she expected this response because she figured that not only everyone in this town, but also everyone from neighboring lands would have heard of this impressive monument.

"I don't know if it has a name," the man replied, "but we are in the land of Shinar, if that answers your question."

Whitney was baffled. She was sure

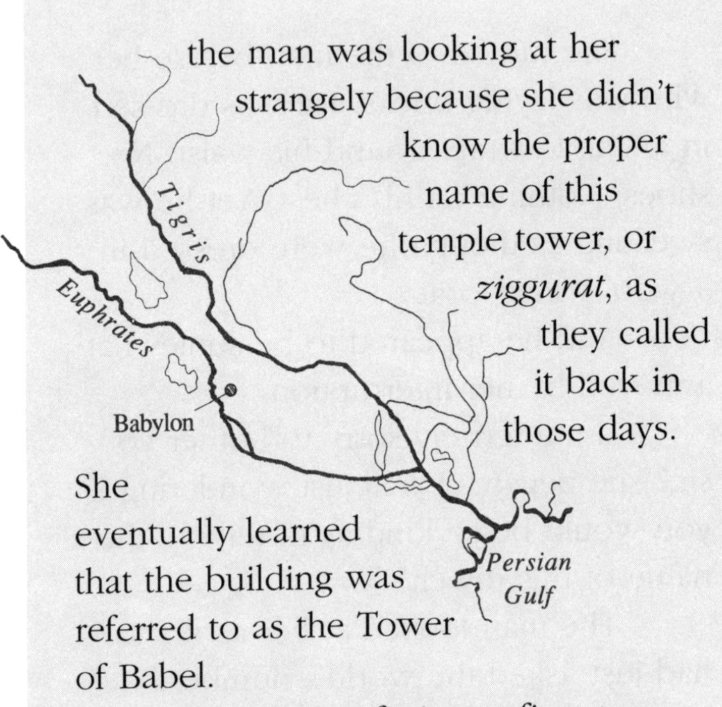

the man was looking at her strangely because she didn't know the proper name of this temple tower, or *ziggurat*, as they called it back in those days.

She eventually learned that the building was referred to as the Tower of Babel.

This was confusing at first, too, because she had heard of the land of Babylonia, but not Babel. She wondered if the two were related. Later she learned that *Babel* is the Hebrew word for *Babylon*, which the people understood to mean the "gate of God." Babel is thought to have been the ancient city of Babylon, the capital of the Babylonian empire.

The city of Babylon stood on the Euphrates River, in what is now southern Iraq. Back before the natives knew this land as Babylonia, they called it Shinar.

Since the city was later to be called Babel, the "gate of God," it was fitting that its tower stretched to the heavens.

CHAPTER THREE

ON TOP OF THE WORLD

"Coming through, coming through," two men yelled to Whitney and Bailey, as they passed by carrying a heavy handbarrow loaded with mud bricks. From where she stood, it looked as if the tower was nearly complete. However, she overhead some workers discussing all the labor that still needed to be done.

"We are only a little more than halfway there," one man said to the others with a look of exhaustion.

"No, we are at least two-thirds of the way through," another countered.

"Well, no matter who is right, we

still have much to do, and there is no point of arguing about it," a third man reasoned.

"Yeah, but it will be well worth it," said a young worker laying bricks beside the men. "After the tower is done, we will be closer to God than any other people, and every land far and wide will envy us. They will want to be like us and have towers of their own, but they

won't know how to build them."

"It's true," added the exhausted man who had spoken first. "There is no denying that we are the smartest and most efficient city in Mesopotamia. After the temple tower is complete, we will be the holiest, too."

"Just think," continued the young man. "At the top of our tower we will be able to observe all of the other cities baking their own mud bricks and beginning the construction of their own tiny towers. And we will laugh as we enjoy our food and drink and relax."

"And what if they come to visit our temple so that they can use it as a model for their own?

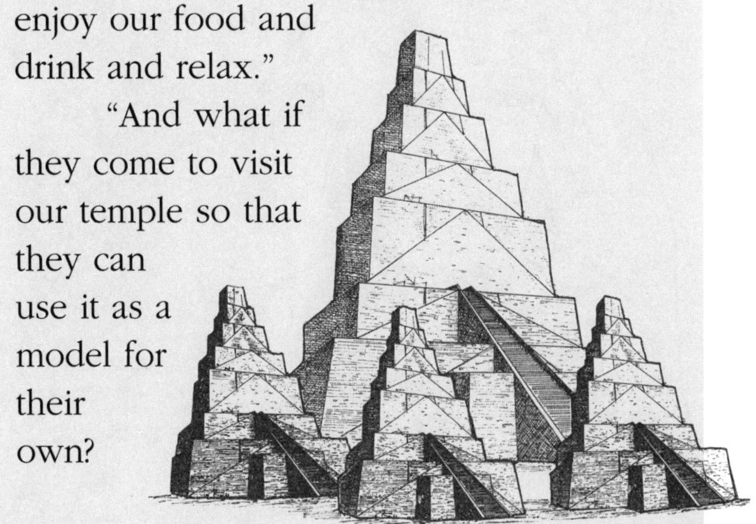

Shall we let them gaze at our magnificence and throw them out before they copy our design? Or should we wait until they question us about our method and then pretend as though we don't understand?"

The men laughed until their bellies ached and until they got reprimanded for goofing off on the job.

"Enough of that talk! Get to work!" a supervisor yelled to them from the fourth tier of the tower.

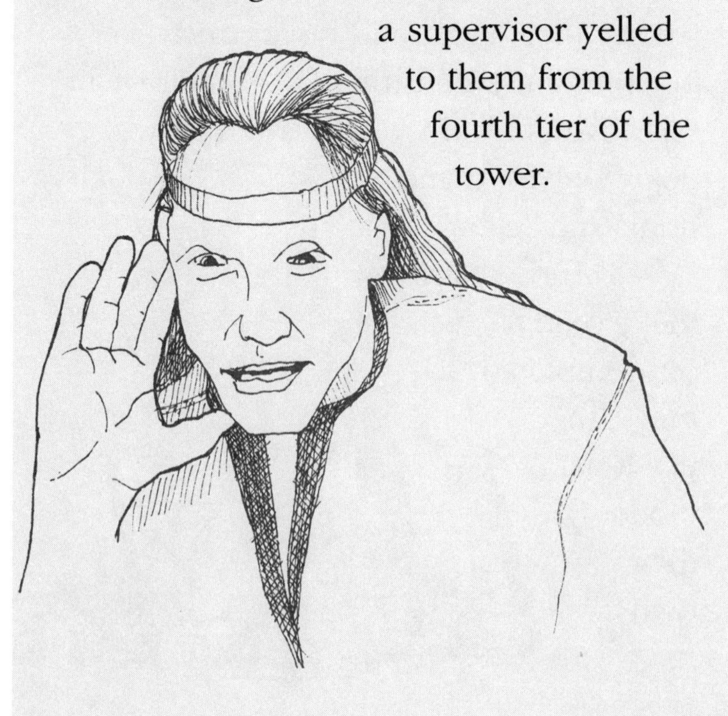

Whitney recognized the sarcasm in the men's voices. It was the same tone she had used earlier that day when she asked her soccer buddies whether they thought the Ravens might have a chance at winning the championship if Whitney's team didn't use their goalie. And it was the same tone Tonya and Nicki used when they added their comments about scoring a goal or two for the competition and waiting until the fourth quarter to score any goals at all.

She and her friends were also guilty of an arrogance similar to what she had heard in the men's talk. When she was part of the joking around, she didn't know the remarks sounded so bad. By eavesdropping on a similar conversation, she got to hear what they sounded like from an outsider's point of view. And they were ugly and offensive.

"I guess I can see why Coach Smith was so upset at practice," the soccer star said to her pup with a big sigh. "Too bad these guys don't have someone like Coach to put them in their place."

CHAPTER FOUR

CONFUSION EVERYWHERE

Whitney and Bailey had just reached the sixth terrace of the tower when the efficient system of brick building began to crumble.

"Shem, hand me the jar of tar," said an elderly man next to the ten-year-old and her dog.

"What?" Shem replied.

"Hand me the tar!" the first man yelled back. His words seemed loud and clear to several workers nearby who had heard the request.

But Shem still didn't understand. He walked toward the elderly man with a confused expression on his face.

"I don't understand what you are saying," Shem said.

Now the elderly man was confused. He gawked at Shem as though he had just made up a language of his own.

The two men bantered back and forth, resolving nothing. Trying to mediate between the two, several people joined in, but this only worsened matters. Now half of the people were screaming something to the others, who didn't understand a word of it. Half understood Shem. Half understood the elderly man. But no one understood them both. In a fit of frustration, the two sides started throwing mud bricks at each other.

"You idiot! Why can't you understand these words?"

"What the heck are you saying?"

"Stop babbling!"

Everyone began to speak at once, and it was utter chaos and confusion.

Afraid that she or her dog might get pelted by a brick, Whitney grabbed Bailey and scurried up to the seventh floor. Surely she would be safe there, she thought.

But as soon as the two reached the top of the stairs, it was the same: people yelling and screaming words that made no sense to the others. Moreover, the language on this floor differed from the babble on the lower level. The dialects and inflections were so distinct that the two levels couldn't communicate with each other.

And that was how it was with the entire tower. Each floor spoke two or more languages that no one but a few people could understand. It was like hearing a Russian scream something in his native tongue to a Japanese man, or a German give an order to a group of Spaniards.

Whitney was fascinated by what

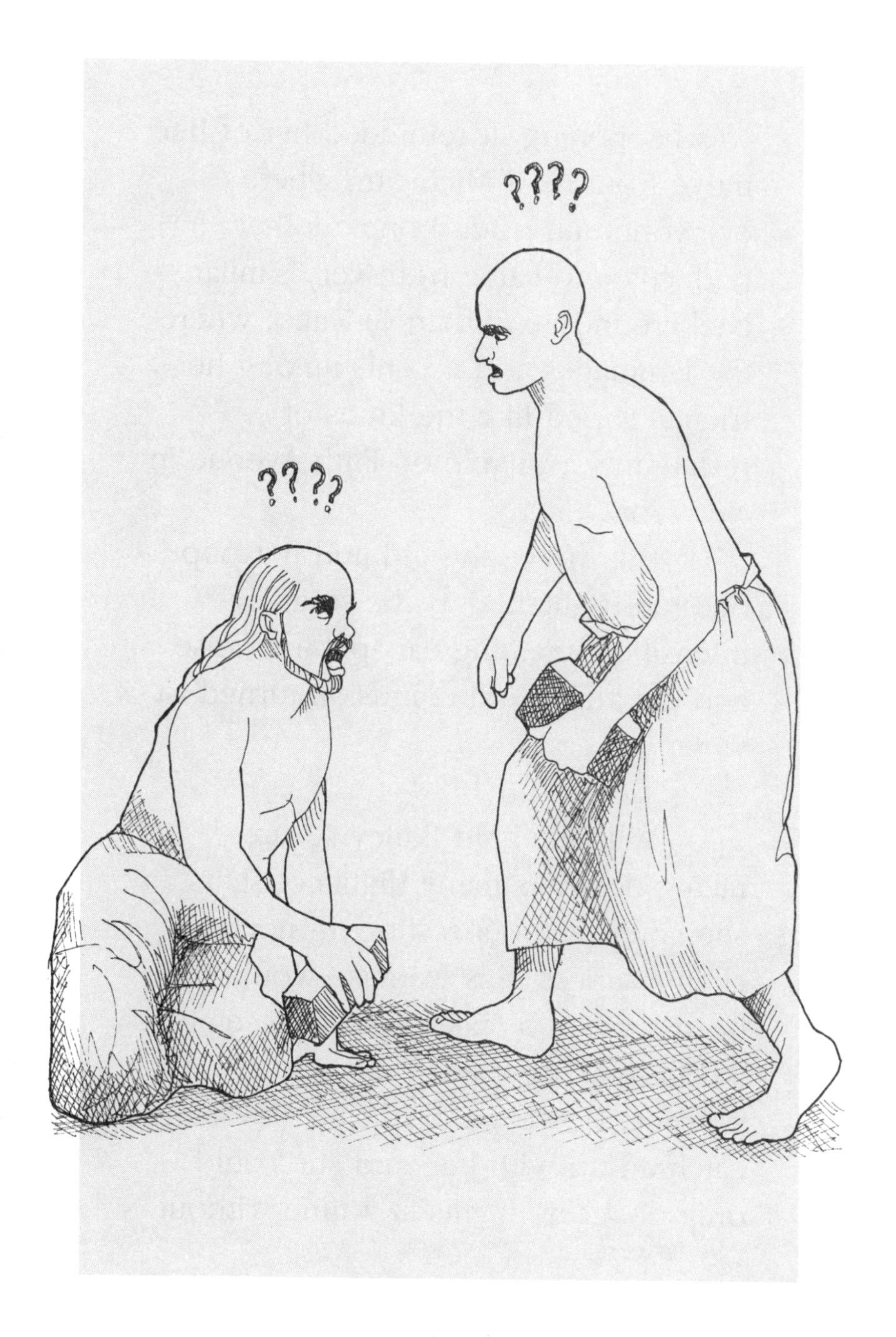

was happening. It reminded her of her move from rural Michigan, where everyone understood one another perfectly and came from very similar backgrounds, to urban Chicago, where the languages and accents among her friends varied like the kinds of restaurants available on Fifth Avenue in New York City.

But the young girl and her pup became frightened as the sound intensified, creating ear-splitting noise, and the anger and confusion turned to violence.

Whitney held Bailey securely, racing down as many flights of stairs as she could without resting. In normal circumstances, this exercise would have been a piece of cake, since it resembled a drill the soccer team did at every practice. However, her laziness was catching up with her, and she could only do a few flights at a time without

losing her breath. Of course, dodging the mud bricks being thrown her way didn't help things.

As soon as the two were at ground level in front of the tower, they rushed out to the mud fields hoping to find some peace and tranquility—and possibly some order. However, the field workers suffered from the same confusion and disorder, even though this group was a little more civilized than the terrace workers. The city was plagued with a universal problem of miscommunication.

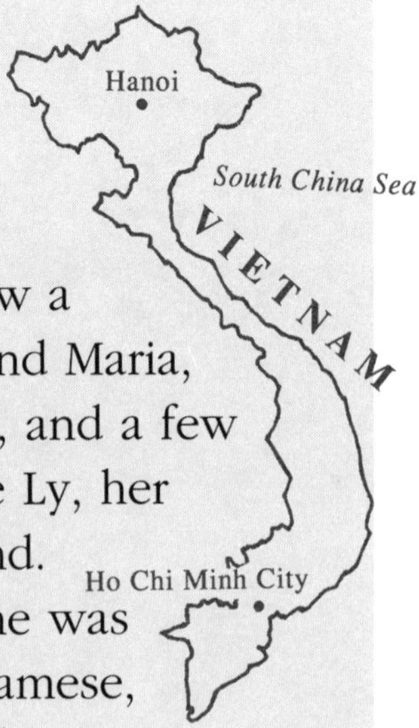

Whitney wished she could be of help. She knew a little Spanish from her friend Maria, who was raised in Mexico, and a few Vietnamese words from Le Ly, her Vietnamese American friend. But she didn't think anyone was speaking Spanish or Vietnamese, or French or German for that matter. The languages all sounded like different versions of the same jumble to her, possibly dialects of Hebrew, Aramaic, Arabic, and Amharic. Too bad the fifth-grader hadn't learned any of these languages yet in school.

Chapter Five

Scattered About

As Whitney looked around her, she noticed many small groups beginning to form. Those who spoke the same language gathered together, until the entire city consisted of thousands of small groups.

"How sad," the ten-year-old thought to herself, "that the people can no longer talk to one another."

Just then darkness covered the sky, and an unmistakable voice—the sound of ultimate wisdom—began to speak.

"I have confused your speech because you, my people, are growing

vain. You think that you can be like God with your tower. But God is almighty and all-knowing.

"You try to distinguish yourselves among other lands with this tower, but by doing so, you refuse to accept your place as humans in a universe governed by God alone.

"Your tower is an act of arrogance. Soon there will be no limit to what you will want and do in the name of pride.

"Therefore I will separate you and scatter you across many lands so as to guard against future assaults on my infinite power."

Silence fell over the entire city. Finally there was order and understanding in the land of Shinar, but with much regret. Families who had been divided into different groups began to wail aloud, and workers who had slaved over the tower for years and years held their heads in their hands in disbelief and disgust.

Gradually workers began to descend from every tier of the tower. Abandoning the handbarrows still loaded with mud bricks and the warm jars of tar, they begrudgingly advanced toward the many flights of stairs.

The procession of workers marching down the layered tower was quite a spectacle. Like solemn soldiers having just lost their war, the men climbed down the many staircases of

their lookout—what was going to be their great achievement.

During the great exodus, Whitney and Bailey wandered the area in search of a group of people whom they could understand. They began by sneaking behind as many groups as they could, eavesdropping on their conversations. But as the people split and traveled different paths, there was more and more distance between the mini-nations, and the task became more difficult.

The scene was like one from a Western movie. As the young girl observed all the people stretched out in every possible direction, she couldn't help but think of the wild West. The people of Shinar weren't dressed in cowboy hats or riding on horses, but they were just as anxious to scout out new land for themselves and to claim it as their own.

After trying out more than fifty groups, the fifth-grader and her dog gave up on their task of finding people with whom they could communicate. After all, they hadn't even gotten to know these people. And from what the young girl was able to understand, she didn't particularly like them.

"Seeing this makes me think that I should get back to soccer practice and do something about our team's attitude," Whitney thought to herself. She feared that winning the championship would become as impossible as this city's building a tower.

She turned to Bailey, her best buddy in the world, and said, "After hearing these people talk, I never want to be a snob again."

But until she got out of Shinar, she couldn't prove her change of attitude. And for that she needed her Emerald Bible.

"Oh Bailey, do you remember

where I left my Emerald Bible? We need Nana's special book in order to get home."

Whitney hadn't even finished her sentence when the handsome lab ran off toward the tower. Trying to keep up with him, the soccer player imagined she was at practice again.

"Discipline and practice," she repeated to herself over and over, remembering what Coach said in his talk with the team.

Once Bailey reached the base of the tower, he ran up three flights of stairs. And there, on the third terrace, lay the beautiful book that reminded the young girl of her beloved grandmother.

She hugged her pup closely to her and congratulated him on a job well done.

Comfortably seated on the steps of the tower with her favorite pet on her lap, she opened her Bible and began to read the last paragraph of the story.

"The people stopped their work and were spread throughout the world. The tower was named Babel, because it was there that God confused the language of all the earth."

Chapter Six

Practice Makes Perfect

As soon as Whitney looked up from reading the last word in the paragraph, she found herself once again seated on Nana's favorite chair with Bailey right beside her.

Curious about the word *babel*, she researched it online and discovered that it comes from the Hebrew verb *balal*, meaning "to confuse" or "to mix."

She was still at the computer looking up exactly where the city of Babel would be in modern Iraq when she heard her mother yell down to her from the kitchen.

"Whitney," she said, "Tonya is on the phone for you."

Whitney quickly picked up the phone that was right next to the computer she had been using in the basement.

"Got it. You can hang up," the young girl yelled back to her mother before saying hello to Tonya. She didn't want Mrs. Bickham to overhear any part of the conversation.

"Whitney," Tonya said, "I feel real bad about what Coach said at practice today."

She continued talking before Whitney had a chance to interject. "And I am a little scared about the big game on Saturday. We are unprepared, Whitney. We might lose our undefeated title if we don't practice really hard this week."

"I know, Tonya, I know," Whitney replied. She agreed wholeheartedly with what her friend had to say. "What do you think we should do to convince Coach that we've changed our attitudes? Should we call him at home?"

"Nah, let's all get to practice early tomorrow. We'll begin the usual drills without his instruction. When he shows up and sees us practicing on our own, he'll know that we have taken his words to heart and that we are ready to work hard."

"Yeah. That's a good plan. Have you got a phone directory of the team there?"

"Yep," Tonya replied. "I'll call all the players whose last names begin with *A* through *M*. You cover *N* through *Z*. Deal?"

"Deal!" Whitney answered. She hung up the phone feeling humbled, not only by what Coach and Tonya had said, but also by what she had learned from the people of Babel.

"I sure hope we win," she told Bailey, who lay asleep next to her, snoring away. "But whether we win or lose, I will never act like a snob again."

ALSO IN
THE EMERALD BIBLE COLLECTION

WHITNEY RIDES THE WHALE
WITH JONAH
and learns she can't run away

Whitney, who has just moved to Chicago, is apprehensive about her first day in fifth grade in a new school. When she opens her Emerald Bible to the story of Jonah and the whale, she is transported there, with Jonah, as she learns a lesson about running away from God and her fears.

ISBN: 0-8091-6663-1
5 1/2" x 8 1/2"   80 pages
$5.95

WHITNEY SEWS JOSEPH'S MANY-COLORED COAT

and learns a lesson about jealousy

Whitney and some friends pull a prank on the "teacher's pet" because they are jealous of her. Through her Emerald Bible Whitney is transported to the story of Joseph and his brothers, where she learns that nothing good comes from jealousy and that different people have different talents and gifts.

ISBN: 0-8091-6664-X
5 1/2" x 8 1/2"   80 pages
$5.95

WHITNEY COACHES DAVID
ON FIGHTING GOLIATH

and learns to stand up for herself

Whitney is up against the school's most popular clique of girls. In fear, she turns to her Emerald Bible and reads the story of David and Goliath, which inspires her to fight her own giant.

ISBN: 0-8091-6669-0
5 1/2" x 8 1/2"   80 pages
$5.95

WHITNEY SOLVES A DILEMMA
WITH SOLOMON

and learns the importance of honesty

Whitney turns to her Emerald Bible after she is caught cheating on a math test. As she reads from the story of Solomon's judgment, she learns an important lesson about honesty and helps the wise king solve a perplexing dilemma.

ISBN: 0-8091-6668-2
5 1/2" x 8 1/2"   80 pages
$5.95

WHITNEY STOWS AWAY ON NOAH'S ARK

and learns how to deal with peer pressure

Whitney and her fifth-grade science class make fun of a classmate who uses a laptop computer to take copious notes. When the jokes turn cruel, Whitney regrets not standing up for him and turns to her Emerald Bible, where she reads the story of Noah and the flood. As a stowaway on Noah's ark, she learns what to do in the face of mockery.

ISBN: 0-8091-6674-7
5 1/2" x 8 1/2"   80 pages
$5.95

ABOUT THE AUTHOR

Therese Johnson Borchard has always been inspired by the wisdom of the Bible's stories. As a young child, especially, she was intrigued by biblical characters and awed by their courage. She pursued her interest in religion and obtained a B.A. in religious studies from Saint Mary's College, Notre Dame, and an M.A. in theology from the University of Notre Dame. She has published various books and pamphlets in which she creatively retells the great stories of the Judeo-Christian tradition.

ABOUT THE ILLUSTRATOR

Wendy VanNest began drawing as a small, fidgety child seated beside her father at church. He gave her his bulletin to scribble on to help her keep still during the service. People around them began donating their bulletins, asking her for artwork, and at the end of the service, an usher would always give her his carnation boutonniere. As a result of this early encouragement, she pursued her interest and passion in art, and has been drawing ever since.